# The Winter's Tale

Tynnwyd o'r stoc
Withdrawn

Written by William Shakespeare

Retold by Alan Gibbons

Illustrated by Kunal Kundu

## Collins

# Characters

**Antigonus:**
Leontes' chief adviser,
and Camillo's boss

**Leontes:**
King of Sicily

**Hermione:**
Queen of Sicily

**Paulina:**
a servant of Hermione,
and Antigonus's wife

**Mamillius:**
Hermione and
Leontes' son

**Polixenes:** King of Bohemia

**Camillo:** Leontes' adviser

**Prince Florizel:** the son of King Polixenes

**Perdita:** Hermione and Leontes' daughter

**The shepherd**

# 1 An icicle in the heart

This is a tale of life and the ways it can go wrong, of
how love and friendship can be broken and mended.
It tells of cold times and cold hearts. It tells of
the passage of time and how it takes people far from
home, and sometimes, with a little luck, how it can
bring them back.

Our story begins long, long ago in Sicily. At that
time, there was a king whom everybody thought was
wise and just, and his name was Leontes. His queen was
called Hermione, a woman both beautiful and good.

King Leontes and Queen Hermione had a son called
Mamillius, a boy of great promise who'd one day surely
be king himself. To complete the family's happiness,
there was another child on the way and, as if to prove
that life could hardly be better, Leontes and Hermione
had a guest at that time: Polixenes, King of Bohemia.

Leontes and Polixenes had been close
childhood friends. Polixenes' stay had brought warmth
and laughter to the royal household and reminded
both kings of the joys of their childhood. But childhood
passes and boys become men, and the time came for
Polixenes to return home to Bohemia.

"Please stay a little longer," Leontes begged. "Just one more week."

No matter how Leontes pleaded, Polixenes was determined to return home and take care of things there. It was at this moment that Leontes thought of his lovely wife and how she could charm everyone around her.

Hermione advised her husband not to push his friend too hard. She understood that Polixenes was eager to return to his family and see his own young son. However, keen to please her husband, Hermione set about persuading Polixenes on his behalf.

"We'd all like you to stay longer," Hermione said. "I'm not your jailer, but your hostess."

Hermione reminded Polixenes of how long it
had been since they'd shared each other's company.
While Leontes played with his son, Mamillius, he kept
an eye on the conversation. Would his beautiful queen
succeed where he'd failed and win his old friend round?
He watched them as they talked. He noticed every smile
and glance and saw the way they leant in close.

But when Polixenes finally gave in to Hermione's
persuasion, Leontes didn't feel any pleasure. All the time
he'd observed them, he'd felt growing doubts about
what they were doing. It was as if an icicle had entered
his heart and frozen all his good feelings. How had
Hermione been able to succeed in persuading Polixenes
where he'd failed?

Suddenly, all Leontes felt was jealousy.

He found himself staring at his son. In some ways it was like gazing into a mirror. The boy's face was his face. Surely there could be no question that this was his child. A doubt haunted Leontes, however. It was crazy, but it was real. What if Mamillius wasn't his son at all, but Polixenes' child? The icicle of jealousy froze his whole being.

Leontes ushered his son out into the corridor and sent him to his room. Mamillius wondered why his father sounded so cold. Had he done something wrong?

Left alone in the corridor, Leontes paced up and down, driven mad by his crazy thoughts. No matter how he tried, he couldn't stop them. They were like a swarm of bees stinging away at him. He leant against the wall, feeling empty inside. What if his life was a lie and his wife was a woman capable of deceiving him? What if Hermione and Polixenes were at that very moment talking about him behind his back, laughing at him?

Suddenly, he doubted everyone around him. He was surrounded by enemies. He called for one of his advisers, Camillo, and started questioning him.

"Did you hear how quickly Polixenes changed his mind about staying?" Leontes demanded, the doubts still driving him crazy. "How could that happen?"

"That was your good wife Hermione's doing," Camillo said, unaware of the king's jealous thoughts. "She could charm the stars from the sky."

Camillo thought this answer would make Leontes happy, but the king flew into a rage. Now he was more convinced than ever that there was something between his wife and Polixenes. Suddenly, he was suspicious of his adviser too.

Camillo was bewildered by the king's attitude and tried to persuade him he'd nothing to worry about, but the cold, senseless jealousy that had taken over Leontes' mind made it impossible for him to think straight. All he saw was wrong and betrayal. He seemed to have forgotten that it was he who'd asked Hermione to persuade Polixenes to stay.

He turned on his trusted adviser in fury. Hadn't Camillo noticed how slippery his wife was, whispering behind his back with Polixenes? Camillo protested that there was nothing to worry about.

"Is whispering nothing?" Leontes snarled. "They were leaning close to one another, cheek to cheek."

Camillo was horrified at his master's raging and tried to calm him, but nothing worked. Leontes' mind was full of a kind of sickness.

Finally, jealousy turned to thoughts of murder, and Leontes demanded that Camillo poison Polixenes. Camillo was sickened, but knew that if he refused, Leontes would get somebody else to carry out the murder. Somehow he had to prevent his master committing a terrible crime.

"I'll do it, my lord," he said, secretly determined to find some way to save Polixenes. Once the king was gone, Camillo leant against the wall to steady himself as he thought.

"Here he is now," Camillo murmured, seeing Polixenes approaching. How could he tell Polixenes what Leontes was planning? As it turned out, he had his chance. Polixenes had noticed Leontes' change of mood.

"Is the king angry with me?" he asked.

At first, Camillo was unsure how to answer.

"I think you know something, Camillo," Polixenes said. "Let's hear it. What's wrong with the king, your master?"

Camillo wriggled and squirmed, wondering how to tell what he knew. Polixenes demanded that he spit it out. Eventually, Camillo spoke up. "The king's ordered me to murder you," he said.

"Why?" Polixenes cried. "What am I supposed to
have done?"

Camillo heard the wind whipping around the castle
walls and shuddered. "He believes that you and
the queen have betrayed him," he murmured. "You have
to leave this place. I'll come with you."

Polixenes remembered the emotions he'd seen in his
old friend's face, and he knew then that Camillo was
telling the truth. The two men feared for the queen
and for their own lives.

"You're right, Camillo," Polixenes said
at last. "Since I was intending to leave
anyway, my ship's ready to sail.
For everyone's sake, it's time to go."

# 2 A sad tale

The royal prince, Mamillius, was curled up peacefully
next to his mother, Hermione. His head was resting
on her growing tummy. He knew what it meant.
Before long, he'd have a new brother or sister. As he
listened to the whistle of the wind outside, Mamillius
felt warm and secure. He didn't realise that an icy wind
was about to tear his happiness away.

"Tell me a story, Mamillius," said Hermione.
Like Mamillius, she didn't dream that her happy life
was about to fall apart.

"A sad tale's best for winter," Mamillius replied.

But just at this moment, Leontes arrived with his chief adviser Antigonus, Camillo's boss. Leontes' eyes were staring. He'd just learnt that Polixenes had fled with Camillo, and he was furious. In his tormented mind, their disappearance proved that he was being betrayed. He glared at Mamillius and Hermione.

"Get the boy out of here," he growled. "He isn't mine and nor is the queen's unborn child." He wagged a finger at Hermione, his whole body trembling. "You'll never see Mamillius again."

"But why – what's happened?" asked Hermione, astonished and desperate at the thought of being parted from Mamillius.

"You and Polixenes have betrayed me!" thundered Leontes. "You're both traitors – and so is Camillo! Polixenes and Camillo have escaped my anger, fleeing like cowards, but you won't escape!"

At this, Hermione broke down in tears. But to Leontes, this was simply further proof of her guilt. He ordered her to be thrown in prison at once.

Hermione could see that her husband's mind was made up. "I see my fate's settled," she said. "But please let me take my ladies-in-waiting with me. I'll need them, as my baby's soon to be born."

The king granted her wish and ordered her out of his palace.

But Antigonus was worried. "Think who'll suffer," his chief adviser said. "Yourself, your queen, your son and the new baby when it arrives."

But Leontes would have none of it. He was sure Hermione was guilty, and he wanted to convince the rest of the court.

There was one sure way to prove the truth. At the temple of Apollo in Delphi about three weeks' journey away, there was an oracle, a priestess, who revealed the words of the gods. Nobody had ever argued with her verdict. Leontes sent two of his men to ask the oracle for the truth about Hermione and Polixenes.

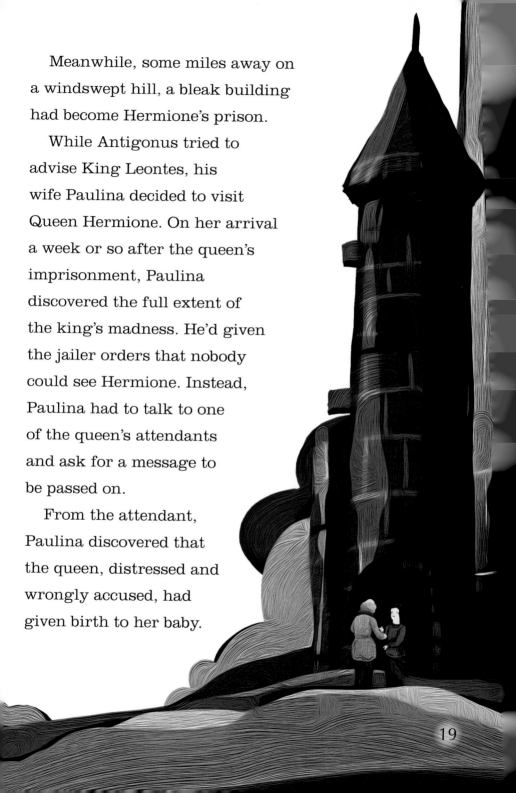

Meanwhile, some miles away on a windswept hill, a bleak building had become Hermione's prison.

While Antigonus tried to advise King Leontes, his wife Paulina decided to visit Queen Hermione. On her arrival a week or so after the queen's imprisonment, Paulina discovered the full extent of the king's madness. He'd given the jailer orders that nobody could see Hermione. Instead, Paulina had to talk to one of the queen's attendants and ask for a message to be passed on.

From the attendant, Paulina discovered that the queen, distressed and wrongly accused, had given birth to her baby.

"A boy?" Paulina asked.

"A healthy baby girl," came the answer. "You should've heard what the queen said. 'My poor prisoner, I'm as innocent as you.'"

Paulina knew what she had to do. She sent her message to Hermione. She'd take the newborn baby girl to the king. Surely, if he saw his daughter, his heart would soften and he'd come to his senses. How could he reject his own child? Persuading the jailer to let her go with the child, Paulina set off for the king's court.

Back in the palace, the king hadn't been able to sleep. He was still brooding about the queen's betrayal. His court had become a sad, lonely place in her absence, quiet and empty, with no sound of laughter. His son Mamillius had taken the jailing of his mother badly and was gravely ill. Leontes was worried about the boy, but he was still obsessed with the idea that he'd been wronged.

At that moment, Paulina arrived, carrying Hermione's baby daughter. "I come from the queen," she said. "My lord, your wife has given birth to a baby girl. She's your daughter."

Very gently, Paulina laid the baby down on a table before Leontes. Surely he'd recognise the child as his? Instead, the sight of the child sent the king into yet another fit of rage and he demanded that Paulina leave.

"You're mad," Paulina said, unable to believe his reaction. "The queen's innocent and this is your child."

Nothing could make Leontes listen. He ranted and paced the floor, calling his court a nest of traitors.

Still, Paulina tried to persuade him. She pointed out the baby's features. "She's just like you: her frown, her dimples, every bit of her face."

Leontes was so furious he threatened to have Paulina burnt like a witch. With great courage, Paulina struggled on, trying to get the king to see sense.

"Look at the baby, my lord," she said. "She's yours."

When Leontes still wouldn't accept the baby as his, Paulina departed, leaving the baby with the king. He drew away from the little girl as though she were something horrible, and turned to Antigonus. "Take the child away," he said. "Leave her in some desert or wilderness to die."

Barely able to believe the king's words, Antigonus gently picked up the baby. As cruel as the king's decision was, Antigonus was his loyal servant and he knew he had to follow orders. Unlike his wife Paulina, he would never go against his master's wishes.

Leontes watched Antigonus depart with the baby and grunted, "I won't raise another man's child."

Just then he got some news. His men had returned from Delphi with the oracle's decision. It was time for the truth.

# 3 The oracle's verdict

In the palace, the court of justice assembled to hear the oracle's verdict. Horns brayed. Drums beat. The great lords and ladies made their way inside to discover Queen Hermione's fate.

Last to enter was the most powerful of them all, their king, Leontes. He took his throne and gestured for everyone to be seated. "Bring in the queen," he ordered. "Let's hear the oracle's decision. You'll see that I'm no tyrant and that I'm telling the truth about my faithless wife."

Hermione stumbled into view, supported by Paulina and her ladies-in-waiting. Still weak so soon after giving birth, she was pale and walked with some difficulty, leaning on the other women.

When everyone was seated, an officer read the charge against the queen, accusing her of conspiring to kill Leontes and marry King Polixenes of Bohemia.

"There's no point in pleading not guilty," Hermione said sadly. She turned to her husband. "Don't you understand, my lord, that I've always been faithful and true?"

Leontes was unmoved. "Criminals always say they're innocent," he said, sneering and turning away.

"I only did what you wanted," Hermione protested, "begging Polixenes to stay because he was your friend. As for Camillo, you're treating him unfairly. He's a good and honest man."

At this, Leontes snorted angrily. "You must have known Camillo was planning on leaving with Polixenes," he said. "You've betrayed me. Let's hear what the oracle says."

The court officer broke the wax seal on the scroll from the oracle, and read the judgement.

"Hermione's innocent," he announced, "and Polixenes too. Camillo's a true and loyal servant." A gasp ran around the court. The oracle had found against the king. "The king's a jealous tyrant," the officer continued, "and he'll have no other children, no heir to the throne, if that which is lost isn't found."

Paulina sighed. That had to mean the baby girl she'd brought to court was now lost.

As one, the lords and ladies turned to look at the king. It was time for Leontes to admit his mistake and forgive his queen. Leontes did nothing of the kind. He snatched the scroll and stared at it in disbelief.

"Did you read out the truth?" he demanded.

"I did, my lord," the officer said.

After a moment's hesitation, Leontes crumpled
the scroll in his fist and threw it to the floor.
"The oracle's a lie," he thundered. "The queen's trial
will continue."

All around the court, the great lords and ladies
swapped glances. The king was defying the gods.
Before the trial could continue, a servant stumbled
through the door.

"What are you doing, bursting in like this?"
Leontes demanded.

The servant was trembling with fright.

"I've sad news," the servant stammered. "It's Mamillius, your son. He's dead."

The terrible news was too much for the queen. Hermione swayed and fainted.

Leontes stared into midair for a long time. Slowly, his madness started to melt away, the way snow thaws in spring. A terrible pain gnawed at him, more bitter than the fiercest frost. "The god Apollo's angry," he said, shame and sorrow in his voice. "I called his oracle a lie. This is my punishment." He thought of his dead son Mamillius and the baby daughter he'd abandoned. He'd had such a beautiful life and he'd destroyed it in a fit of madness.

Paulina stared at him as she held the queen in her arms. "Do you see what you've done, my lord?" she cried. "Grief's killing her. Don't punish her any more. Let me take her away and tend to her."

"Yes," Leontes said, crushed by what he'd done. Hermione, his queen, was all he had left. "Take her away," he said. "I can't bear any more of this torture. Treat her and bring her back to health." He watched Paulina and the ladies leave with the unconscious queen.

Paulina looked back at him. Could she ever trust this man again after what he'd done?

Overcome with grief, Leontes begged forgiveness from the oracle. Nothing could bring poor Mamillius back to life, but he'd apologise to Polixenes and try to win back the love of his queen. He'd recall Camillo to his court. He'd do all he could to put things right.

Yet there was no easy happy ending for Leontes and those he'd wronged. Even as he announced to his court that he'd put things right, Paulina reappeared, eyes blazing with accusation. "Your queen is dead, tyrant," she cried. "You've brought this upon yourself."

Brokenhearted, Leontes hung his head. "Take me to the dead bodies of my queen and son," he said, his voice wintry with despair.

Meanwhile, far away in Bohemia, Antigonus had arrived with the baby girl. He'd become fond of her on the long journey, and his heart sank at the idea of leaving her alone in the wilderness. But he knew he had to carry out Leontes' orders. He wrapped the baby in her rich golden blanket, and placed her gently in the shelter of some trees. "My heart bleeds for you, little one. Farewell."

He was about to leave the baby to her fate, when he heard a loud roar. To Antigonus's horror, a huge wild bear was lumbering towards him. He saw its terrible jaws and fled for his life.

A few minutes later, a shepherd appeared and came across the abandoned child. The baby was dressed in rich clothing, and tucked into the folds of her blanket were jewels that could make the shepherd rich for the rest of his life. While the shepherd examined the baby, wondering why she'd been left in this wilderness when she obviously came from a wealthy family, his son appeared.

"I've seen a terrible thing," he reported. "A nobleman was attacked by a bear. It was horrible to see."
The shepherd's son told how the bear had sunk its teeth into Antigonus's shoulder and torn him apart.

The shepherd heard him out; then he took the baby in his arms. "I'll call you Perdita – the lost one," he said.

Antigonus might be gone, but Perdita still had someone to watch over her.

# 4 The shepherd's daughter

Our lives are short. Sometimes it seems as if they last no longer than a snowflake melting on your cheek. Sixteen years seemed to pass almost as quickly as the fading snow, but Leontes was tormented by sorrow and remorse. He never forgot that he'd killed his wife and children and falsely accused his friends, Polixenes and Camillo. So much sadness is enough to break a man.

Yet life goes on. The seasons pass. The days lengthen and shorten. Unknown to Leontes, his daughter Perdita had grown up in Bohemia as the daughter of the shepherd who found her.

Life had been good to Perdita. She had grace and beauty, and she attracted the attention of Prince Florizel, King Polixenes' son. It didn't matter to Florizel that Perdita was a poor shepherd's daughter. She'd won his heart and he was determined to marry her. He even disguised himself as a poor farmer, in order to avoid making the shepherd suspicious.

King Polixenes was furious when he heard that his son had fallen in love with a poor shepherd's daughter. It could only mean trouble. He called on his old friend and adviser, Camillo.

"We'll disguise ourselves," Polixenes told Camillo, "and see how things stand with Florizel and this shepherd girl."

At the shepherd's cottage, Florizel and Perdita were happy. They were in love, but love could be dangerous. The royal family wasn't meant to mix with the poor. Perdita was afraid King Polixenes would find out about them.

"What if your father passed this way?" she said. "Imagine if he found out about us. What would he say?" She dropped her voice. "What would he do?"

Of course, the king and his adviser Camillo were already there, spying on the young couple. "This is the prettiest shepherdess I've ever seen," Polixenes whispered to Camillo.

Not knowing that his father was listening, Florizel declared his love for Perdita, and she admitted that she felt the same way.

When the old shepherd came in and heard that they were in love, he was delighted and announced that they should be married. "Hold hands," he said, eyes sparkling with pride and joy.

Polixenes decided that the moment had come to make an appearance. Still in disguise, he and Camillo knocked at the cottage door and asked for a drink of water. It was easy to steer the conversation around to the happy couple.

"Congratulations! But don't you have a father?"
Polixenes asked Florizel. "Shouldn't he be told that
you plan to marry?" He wanted to know if his son was
obedient, or if he'd go against his father's wishes.

"He isn't going to know," Florizel answered.

"Oh, he must," Polixenes insisted, trying to hide
his feelings.

When Florizel continued to refuse, Polixenes at last
threw off his cloak and revealed his true identity as
Bohemia's king and Florizel's father. "You'll never marry
this shepherd girl," he said, his face twisted with rage.
"I'll never allow it. I'd scar Perdita's face and ruin her
beauty first."

Polixenes' pride and arrogance blinded him to everything else, and he became as overcome with his own emotions as Leontes had been 16 years earlier. Furious that his son had disobeyed him, Polixenes swept out of the cottage.

Now he knew that Florizel was in fact the prince, the shepherd was afraid. Perdita was worried too. What chance did they have if the king was against them?

"I'll go back to my sheep," Perdita said, "and weep over my impossible love."

"Well, I'm not afraid," Florizel said. "I won't let my father keep us apart."

Camillo, who knew the king well, advised Florizel to stay out of his sight, at least until the king's current mood had passed. After all, the king had a terrible temper.

After much thought, Camillo finally came up with a plan. Florizel and Perdita had to get away from King Polixenes. Camillo himself had become homesick for Sicily. He'd been away for 16 long years, and was keen to see his old home again – he even hoped that Leontes might have had a change of heart, and be ready to apologise and welcome him back. So he thought of a way of killing two birds with one stone.

"We should flee to Sicily," he told Florizel and Perdita. "We can take refuge there." Camillo suggested that Florizel swap clothes with a passing traveller, to keep his identity secret. With Perdita, they fled down to the shore to find a ship to carry them away to Sicily. The old shepherd, concerned about the girl he'd raised since she was a baby, overheard what they were planning, and decided to follow them.

# 5 A statue comes to life

Sicily's where our tale started and there it'll end. For 16 long years, Leontes had brooded in his palace, unable to forgive himself for his unreasonable jealousy. He found no joy in the world. Hermione had been the perfect wife and queen and he'd destroyed her, and his innocent son Mamillius too.

"It's true," said Paulina, the queen's faithful servant. "If you searched the whole world over, you'd never find anyone to compare with her."

The king nodded sadly. "I won't marry again. Since both my son and my daughter are dead through my fault, I'll have no heir."

While they were talking, news came that
Prince Florizel had arrived at court with Perdita.
Leontes welcomed Florizel warmly as the son of his old
friend Polixenes, and Florizel introduced Perdita as
his wife.

"I had two children," Leontes said, with a deep sigh
of regret, "a boy and a girl. Had they lived, they'd have
been about your age."

Before long, Leontes received further news. The man
he'd betrayed, King Polixenes, had followed his son to
Sicily and was also on his way to court.

"Your father, Florizel!" Perdita cried in shock. "Now
our marriage will never happen!"

"So you're not married, after all?" Leontes said.

Just at this moment, there was a new arrival at court – the old shepherd, who'd followed Perdita and Florizel on their journey.

"What brings you here, old man? How do you know Perdita?" Leontes demanded, seeing Perdita's shock when the old man appeared.

"She's my daughter," he said. "Well, as good as. I found baby Perdita 16 years ago and raised her as if she was my own child. This gem is the last remaining one of the jewels I found in the folds of her blanket." The shepherd held out a gem, and Leontes recognised it at once. It had belonged to his wife. His heart filled as he realised his daughter had returned, as if from the dead.

As the truth began to emerge, Florizel begged for
the king's help. "Will you help me, my lord?" he said.
"If you explain Perdita's royal heritage, perhaps he'll
agree to our marriage."

"I'll meet King Polixenes," Leontes said, "and see what
I can do."

When the two kings finally set eyes on each other,
it was as if 16 years melted away. Leontes apologised
to his old friend with tears of sorrow and shame,
and Polixenes forgave him with the greatest joy.
When everything was finally explained, Polixenes
happily agreed to the young people's marriage.

At last our long, sad tale is coming to
an end. It'll conclude in the deserted house
where Queen Hermione had been kept captive.
Strangely, faithful Paulina had visited this
empty building twice a day, every day, over
the years. What could have brought her so
often to these echoing walls where the wind
howled and wailed like a lost soul?

The main players in our story were
gathered in this deserted house now –
Leontes and Polixenes, Perdita and her
love Florizel, Camillo and Paulina.

All was revealed when Paulina
showed them the secret of
the house: a statue of Queen
Hermione, a thing of wonder.

Paulina drew the curtain
to reveal the statue, which
seemed to glow with life.

"The likeness is amazing,"
said Leontes. "Though
my wife was younger
than this, and she didn't
have these wrinkles."

48

Paulina reached for the curtain, but Leontes begged to look at the statue a little longer. He wanted to roll back time to when life was sweet, and kiss his wife.

Finally, Paulina remembered the good there'd been in Leontes before jealousy started to eat away at him. She pitied him now. "Well," she said slowly, "if you're truly sorry for your past actions, and if you truly wish it, I can use magic to bring Hermione's statue to life."

"Do it," Leontes said, eyes glittering with excitement. "Bring her to life if you can. Nobody will move."

At this moment, magic was in the air. Soft music echoed around the walls that had been silent so long.

"Come to life, statue," Paulina said. "Be stone no more." At Paulina's command, the statue of Hermione stirred. For a moment, her eyes lingered on Perdita. Did they flicker with faint recognition? Slowly, gracefully, Hermione began to descend the steps. As if in a dream, the king reached out to take her hand – and started with surprise. The hand he was touching felt nothing like cold stone.

"She's warm!" Leontes cried. Suddenly, the spell cast by time was broken, and Leontes held Hermione in his arms.

Polixenes watched and gasped out loud. "We've stolen her back from the dead," he said.

Paulina had more news for Hermione, perhaps the greatest news of all. "Turn round, Hermione," she said. "You recognised Perdita, didn't you? You saw something of yourself in her. Yes, she's your long-lost child, whom you haven't seen since she was an innocent baby."

At last, Hermione found her voice. "Where've you been living all these years?" she asked in wonder.

"Explanations can wait," Paulina said. "The wrongs of the past have been put right. Be happy, everyone." Paulina was sad for herself, of course. Faithful as she'd been, she'd no reward other than seeing everyone happy. "Leave me now," she said, "and enjoy your happiness."

At this, Leontes realised that it was time to be a true king and not a tyrant. He could look at his wife Hermione and his friend Polixenes and feel no jealousy. His daughter would be married to Polixenes' son Florizel. This was a time when nobody should be sad.

Leontes brought his adviser Camillo forwards, a friend again 16 years after fleeing the palace in terror. He took Paulina's hand. "You deserve happiness, faithful Paulina," he said. "You'll marry Camillo here." Leontes' eyes travelled from face to face and he smiled. "There'll be time later for us to talk," he said, "and fill in the gaps left by time."

So that's our tale of life and the ways it went wrong, of how love and friendship were broken. Time passed, as time does, like winter rain gliding across the sky. It took people far from home, before bringing them back so that their broken hearts could be mended.

# Causes and consequences

Leontes is jealous
and wants revenge
on Polixenes
and Hermione.

Hermione is
sent to prison.
Mamillius becomes
ill and dies.

Hermione's baby,
Perdita, is sent
away to Bohemia.

Perdita is found by
a shepherd. She grows
up and falls in love with
Polixenes' son, Florizel.

Polixenes leaves
Sicily, taking Camillo
with him. They go
to Bohemia.

Paulina uses magic to turn Hermione into a statue.

Mamillius's death causes Hermione to die of grief.

Polixenes follows them, and everyone ends up back in Sicily. When they all forgive each other, Hermione's statue comes back to life.

Florizel and Perdita escape to Sicily.

Polixenes is cross that Florizel wants to marry a shepherdess.

# Ideas for reading

Written by Clare Dowdall, PhD
Lecturer and Primary Literacy Consultant

**Reading objectives:**
- draw inferences such as inferring characters' feelings, thoughts and motives from their actions, and justify inferences with evidence
- predict what might happen from details stated and implied
- discuss and evaluate how authors use language, including figurative language, considering the impact on the reader

**Spoken language objectives:**
- participate in discussions, presentations, performances, role play, improvisations and debates

**Curriculum links:** PSHE – health and well-being (feelings)

**Resources:** pens and paper; space for drama.

## Build a context for reading
- Talk about an occasion when you've felt jealous and ask children to think about a time when they've felt jealous.
- Share experiences, discussing how jealousy can feel and what it can lead to.
- Look at the covers and read the title and blurb. Discuss what the phrase "time and love can work a strange magic" might mean in this story by William Shakespeare.

## Understand and apply reading strategies
- Turn to pp2–3. Help children to read the characters' names, and to work out how they're related to each other.
- Look at the chapter heading and first paragraphs on p4. Challenge children to work out how the author has used icy imagery and what effect they're trying to create.